C.R. MUDGEON

by Leslie Muir

pictures by
Julian Hector

Atheneum Books for Young Readers

New York London Toronto Sydney New Delhi

For Leo, with love
—L. M. (a.k.a. Mommy)

For Diane Salem and Pat Hector
—J. H.

ATHENEUM BOOKS FOR YOUNG READERS
An imprint of Simon & Schuster Children's Publishing Division
1230 Avenue of the Americas, New York, New York 10020
Text copyright © 2012 by Leslie Muir
Illustrations copyright © 2012 by Julian Hector
ATHENEUM BOOKS FOR YOUNG READERS is a registered trademark of Simon & Schuster, Inc.
For information about special discounts for bulk purchases, please contact Simon &
Schuster Special Sales at 1-866-506-1949 or business@simonandschuster.com.
The Simon & Schuster Speakers Bureau can bring authors to your live event. For more
information or to book an event, contact the Simon & Schuster Speakers Bureau at
1-866-248-3049 or visit our website at www.simonspeakers.com.
Book design by Ann Bobco
The text for this book is set in Fairfield Light.
The illustrations for this book are rendered in charcoal and watercolor.
Manufactured in China
1211 SCP
First Edition
10 9 8 7 6 5 4 3 2 1
Library of Congress Cataloging-in-Publication Data
Muir, Leslie.
C. R. Mudgeon / Leslie Muir ; illustrated by Julian Hector. — 1st ed.
p. cm.
Summary: Hedgehog C. R. Mudgeon, who is used to having everything exactly the same
every day, has some adjusting to do when a lively new neighbor moves into the tree next
door.
ISBN 978-1-4169-7906-7 (hardcover)
[1. Neighbors—Fiction. 2. Hedgehogs—Fiction. 3. Squirrels—Fiction.] I. Hector, Julian,
ill. II. Title.
PZ7.M8838Cr 2012
[E]—dc22   2011006639

A person born to be a flowerpot will not go beyond the porch.

—Mexican proverb

C. R. Mudgeon ate the same supper every single night.

 Celery root soup—no salt.

A cup of dandelion tea—no lemon.

On Tuesdays he picked one small fig for dessert—

but only on Tuesdays.

Every night he snuggled his hedgehoggity feet into his woolly slippers. He sat in the same old chair. He wore the same soft raveled sweater. And he read his favorite book—*Medical Cures from A to Z*—by the crackle of a single twig.

C. R. Mudgeon liked things to stay the same.
So on Tuesday, as always, he set off to go fig picking.
That's when everything changed.

When C. R. Mudgeon stepped out of his hole, he couldn't believe his eyes. He almost tripped. Poppies were planted everywhere, like a carpet of red polka dots.
He followed them.

They led to a mailbox.
It announced loudly:

Someone new had moved in.
The shutters were scarlet;
the swing, sangria. Even the door was red.

He knocked.

"A neighbor!"
said a bright-eyed squirrel
in gardening gloves.
"A friend."

"About those poppies . . ."

"I'm glad
you like them!"
she said.

"They're growing wild.
I'm seeing spots."

"Wonderful!" she exclaimed. "Red spots are *so* cheerful. I hope you like cherry tomatoes. I'm off to plant a bazillion near your door!"

C. R. Mudgeon went home to consult his medical book.

He thought it best to take a nap.

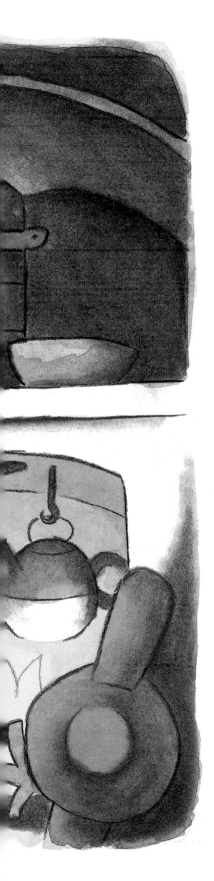

At suppertime C. R. Mudgeon smelled something strange.

Peppery.

Tickly.

He sneezed.

Paprika was cooking. The air was thick with her spices.

C. R. Mudgeon sipped his celery root soup. His nose crinkled. "This soup tastes thin, pale." He scowled over the edge of his bowl—he could see straight to the bottom. He tipped it and took one long slurp. "This just won't do," he muttered.

C. R. Mudgeon knocked on his neighbor's door.

"Miss Paprika,"
he complained,
"your spices are watering
down my soup."
He held out his bowl.

She peered in.
"Oh, dear. This soup has the droops.
I've just the thing!"

She handed him a small bottle:

"One dash will wake up your soup like a snake at a square dance!" she said.

C. R. Mudgeon
sniffed the bottle.
A tickle shot up
his nose.

He sneezed himself into a ball
and rolled right back
down his hole.

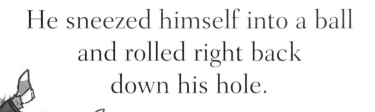

He couldn't unwind
until bedtime.

He put a clothespin on his nose, and went to bed.

The next day C. R. Mudgeon
found a pair of maracas
with a note by his door.

"I do *not* want a friend," he grumbled. He shook a maraca. "Sounds like a box of nuts." He tried to pry it open. "Nuts that you can't even eat." He kicked the maraca and stubbed his toe.

That night he settled into his chair to read.
Suddenly . . .

Thumpety-thump! Then . . .

Bumpety-bump!

Trumpets blared.

Guitars strummed.

Then *bonk!*
A clump of ceiling
fell on his head.

C. R. Mudgeon marched straight over to Paprika's Place.
He knocked.
"Our maraca man is here!" Paprika cheered.
He held out the clump. "I am *not* here to shake my maracas."
Paprika winked. "You'll shake them when you hear our music!"
The band members played on.

C. R. Mudgeon turned chili-pepper red.

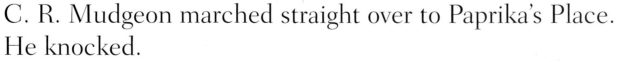

He stomped home
with his clump and
a bump on his head.

Cure for a clump and bump

Hide under a helmet

He put on his
bicycle helmet and
scribbled a letter.

Enough was too much.

Dear Miss Paprika,

1. Your poppies are trespassing.

2. Too many spices spoil the soup.

3. Loud music hurts my head.

Please move to a faraway tree.

Good-bye,
C. R. Mudgeon

He slipped the letter into Paprika's mailbox. He felt much better.

The next night no spices filled the air. His soup tasted boring, anyway.

Paprika's tree was dark and still. The quiet gave him a headache.

The next morning her poppies wilted. Had she moved away?

C. R. Mudgeon knocked at her door. The door creaked open.

Paprika drooped like the poppies.
"I have the whooping whiffles,"
she said.

He tucked her into bed and hurried home.

C. R. Mudgeon knew
just what to do.
He made celery root soup.
"With a smidgen of salt,"
he said.

Next he brewed dandelion tea.
"A touch of lemon, I think."
He added five enormous squeezes.

Then he found it:
the plumpest, sweetest,
most perfect fig.

He headed straight to Paprika's house.

Before he knocked,
he peeked into her mailbox.
His good-bye letter
was still there.

He hid it
in his watch pocket.

Paprika tasted the celery root soup.
Her whiskers fainted.

"Do you like it?"
C. R. Mudgeon asked.

She sat very still, for a squirrel.
"Very rooty,"
she said with a cough.

Paprika sipped the dandelion tea.

"Good?" he asked.

"And tart," she sputtered.

Then she bit into the sweet, juicy fig. Paprika wiggled her whiskers and sat up in bed.

"I feel better already! You're a good friend, C. R."

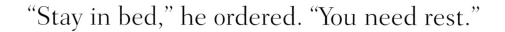

"Stay in bed," he ordered. "You need rest."

"No rest. Mariachi! Tonight!" said Paprika.
"Please come, C. R. Good friends are the spice of life."

So ever after, every Tuesday, he picked the sweetest fig and brought it to mariachi band practice.

And C. R. Mudgeon learned to shake his maracas.

THE END